# KRAKEN

## I

*Necronomicon for children*
by Ismail ibn Abdullah Alhazredî
Copyright © 2020, by Fabio Larcher
All rights reserved
Pictures and graphic project by the author
Translate by Silvia Rossini

NON È MORTO CIÒ CHE RUSSA IN ETERNO:
* STA SOLO DORMENDO *

ISMAIL IBN ABDULLAH ALHAZREDÎ

COMPLETO DI RITUALI ED EVOCAZIONI

NECRONOMICON

PER RAGAZZI

KRAKEN
EDIZIONI

INTRODUTION

*My dear readers, of course, this is N O T a true spell book. I am not really worried about the possibility that you can summon Cthulhu, Dagon, or one of the Outer Gods. There is no risk, simply because there is no a creature like those. Someone should tell you.*

*But imagine they do exist. No one, being of sound mind, would long for their manifestation. They are not like a genius in the bottle, ready to make true the wishes of his summoner. They are monsters that, in the best of cases, would swallow you up and, in the worst one, they would bring Armageddon on the Earth.*

*The* Necronomicon for children, *therefore, is only a fantastic tale, written and illustrated as an act of love for Howard Phillips Lovecraft's work, which has been coming along with me since I was fourteen up to today, following my non-Euclidean lifeline.*

*Writing this book (which can be considered as an introduction to Chtulhu Mythos for beginners or as summary work for experts) was a perfect alibi to work out the pastiche, the prose and the poetry writing and, most of all, the Indian ink drawing.*

*Purists may argue that I took too many liberties,*

*that the sacred texts are not for modifications, and bla bla bla. Maybe a careful reader will notice my subtle disloyalty (or rather, dramatic) to the Master of Providence: I took his works for my personal perusals.*

*Yes, you all are right. I won't hide behind a finger nor a fig-leaf. I used and betrayed Lovecraft. On the other hand, you do this with all Masters. And*

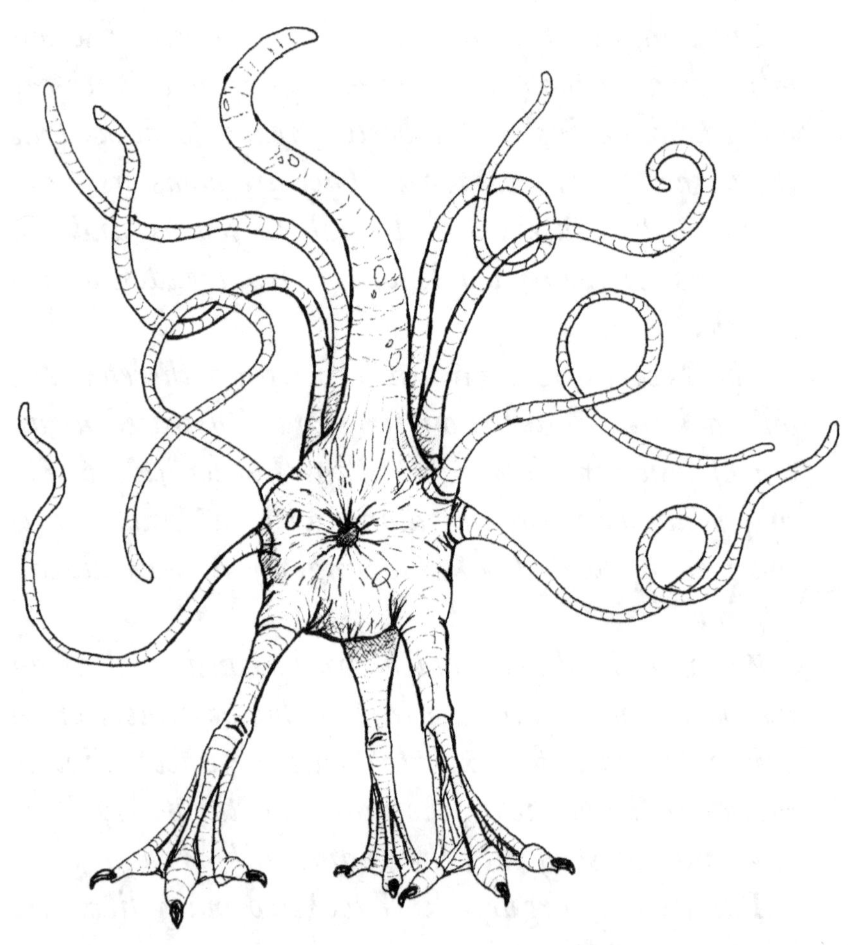

*if Aristotle did the same with Plato, why shouldn't I? What am I? Chopped liver?*

*Is this comparison exaggerated and arrogant? All right, I grant you; but in this way you will never do anything and the world would be really boring (or maybe that concentration camps for political prisoners which it is, come to think of it). Actually, taking liberties is very important for a good purpose and for carrying on the Big Game of imagination and revitalizing symbols and mythos.*

*I am not claiming to be Lovecraft; I am not; but I least I've tried, I've made a contribution, or whatever it means. Be that as it may.*

*Here it is, therefore, my so-called Necronomi-*con for children. *Have a good reading and don't joke! Don't summon Azathoth nor Yog-Sothoth. The world has already enough problems, there is no need to call for the irrational and destructive strengths animating it.*

THE AUTHOR

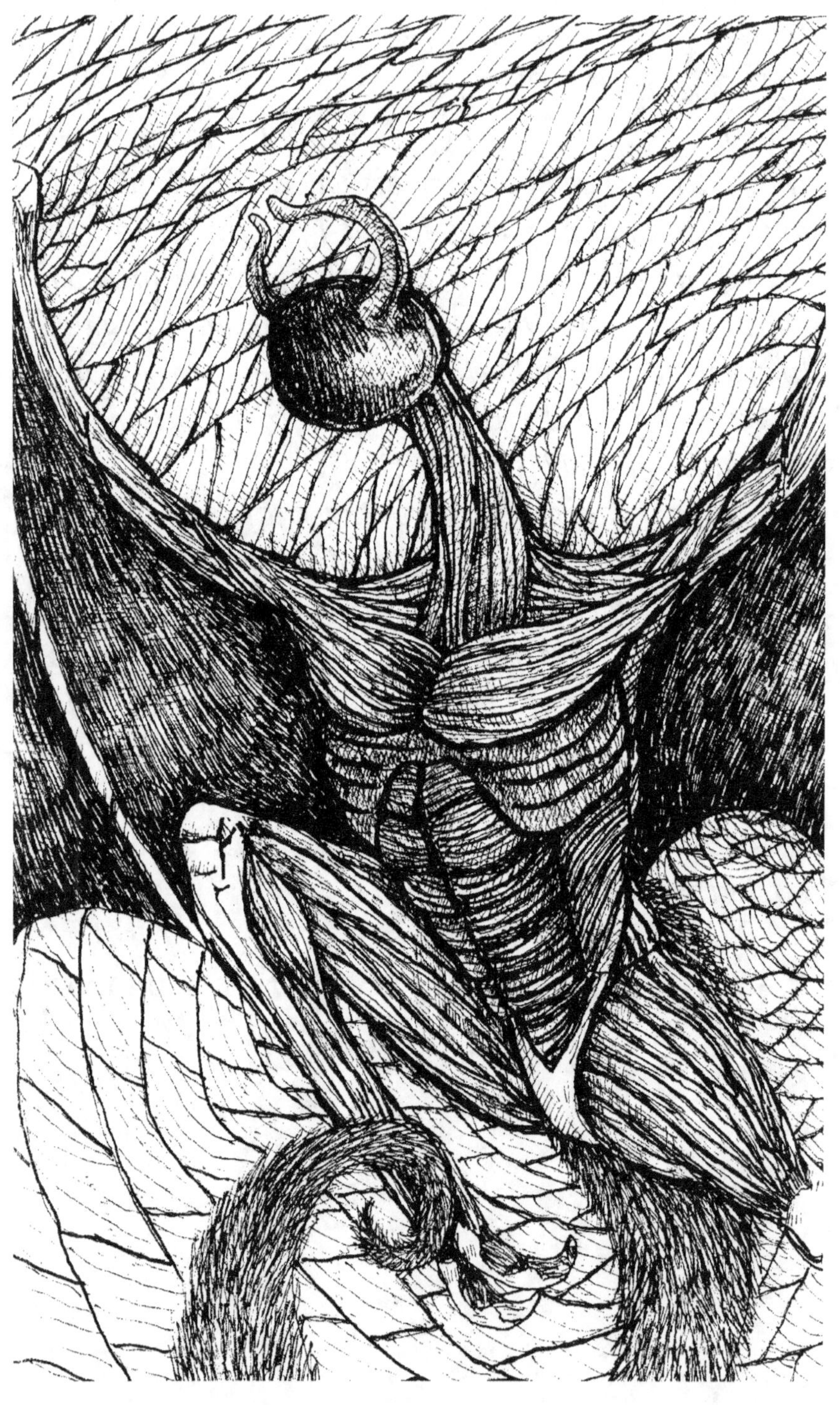

There is only one handwritten specimen of Ismail ibn Abdullah Alhazredî's work. It collects other exoteric texts of different origins, some of them are Hebrew (about magical squares), others from Syria, others from Egypt.

The voluminous in-folio was found by chance from George Angell, professor of Oriental studies at Miskatonic University of Arkham, Massachusetts, in September 1936.

Professor Angell was on a study journey in Baghdad, upon request of his colleague Aloysius Ward, professor emeritus of Archeology, to solve some linguistic ambiguities about a funerary stele of the Omayyad's period.

During a lazy morning, while he was hanging out at the chaotic town market, he noticed the big volume, wrecked by worms and smelling mold and pipe tobacco. He bought it cheap, chased by the old bookseller.

You can imagine his surprise and emotion when, after coming back to his room, he started reading through the old parchment pages: together with odd occultist stuff, he found the story of Ismail, the son of the famous Abdul

Alhazred. This later was the author of the notorious *Necronomicon* (a cursed text, of which the Miskatonic library owned two copies almost intact).

He almost had a stroke.

He spent the night translating the text right away and he always considered this finding as his bigger discovery.

Unfortunately, some fussy colleagues of him detected some differences compared to more accredited alhazaredian sources and other scholars pointed out some small lexical anachronism in the text; therefore, the academic world set Ismail ibn Abdullah Alhazredî's story aside and classified it as a curious literary mystification.

This is the main reason explaining why there is no serious article about this unbelievable tale, which we are publishing for the first time in Italy, except for some specialists and scholars with sense of humor.

Alas, the following text is not a translation of the original. Actually, the old manuscript bought by professor Angell disappeared, maybe stolen for the black market, in October 1961. Jackob Marsh, Miskatonic's librarian, always claimed not being able to explain the theft, despite having been suspected for a long time to be one of the thieves. Suspicions against him were never proved, but he suffered very much for this unfair accusation, both personally and professionally. So that he sent all the university world to Hell, and moved to Innsmouth (his birth town) where he successfully undertook a business in fishing.

He was still in activity at the age of ninety-two; but he suddenly disappeared during a fishing trip with his wrecked fishing boat. His mortal remains were never found and the current rumor is that he did not die, but made a

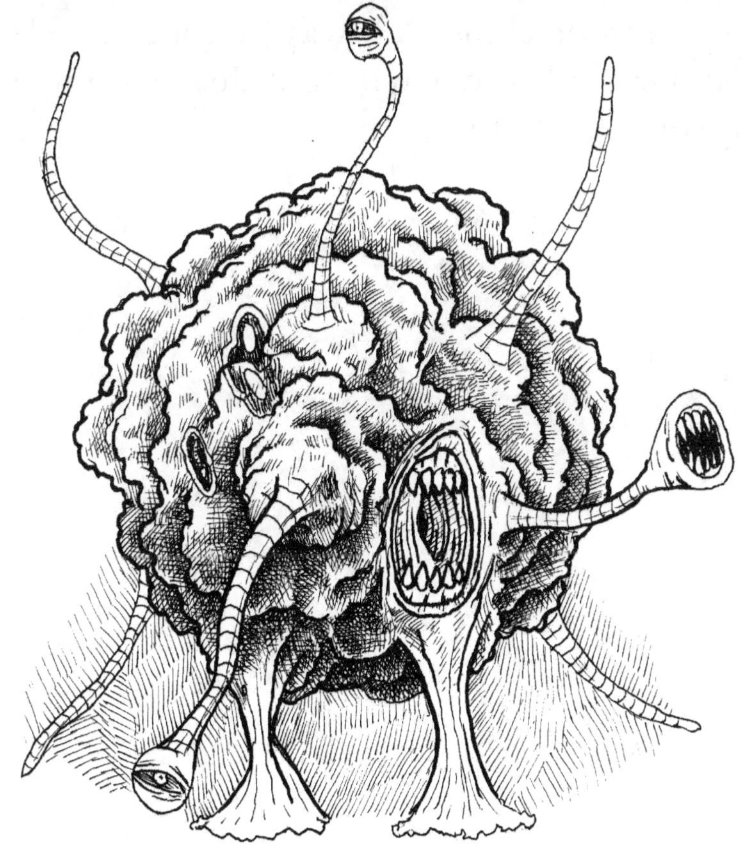

deal with the Deep Ones and he's still living under the sea, serving Dagon. Of course, these are only rumors and we are more likely to believe that he was taken ill, fell outboard and became victim of the several sharks living in these rough but fishy waters.

So we could just to publishing professor Angell's English translation, which was published only one in the U S A : *Necronomicon for children*, Kraken Press Ltd, New York 1949. There are also three unofficial editions, diffused only in some esoteric clubs. Anyway, we are confident that our kind reader will find this text interesting and stimulating.

THE EDITOR

# NECRONOMICON
## FOR CHILDREN

### BY
### ISMAIL IBN ABDULLAH ALHAZREDÎ

aise Allah, Lord of the Worlds, blessed and healthy be our prophet Muhammad, Allah bless him until the Judgement Day. My name is Ismail ibn Abdullah Alhazredî and I am Abdul Alhazred's only son, whom is known as the "Mad Arab", the author of the most important book of dark magic in the world, *Al Azif*.

Maybe you are godless and you only know that terrific book under the Greek name of *Necronomicon*. But that prose translation is full of mistakes and does not fully correspond to my father's content and instructions. Diogenes Hypnoforus, who translated it during Leo the Third's, the Isaurian, reign over Byzantium, disappeared mysteriously, because of his not thorough job. I am afraid that a similar fate will happen to those who will study his erroneous text, while thinking it is correct.

When my father wrote *Al Azif* I was still a child. And when I read it first, I wasn't such older, being not a man, yet. By the way, in its original form it was a poem, but I only dared laying my eyes on that important book after my father's death: he hadn't allowed me to read it because its content was not suitable for a child's mind.

Everyone knows about Abdul Alhazred's death: he was walking in the crowded market of Damascus, in broad daylight, when he was grabbed by an invisible monster and eaten, piece after piece, in front of an incredulous and scared crowd.

Unfortunately, this may happen, when you deal with black magic. Sometimes a small distraction, whispering wrong words, a burred summoning of hell powers is enough to cause a fatality. But you always increase in knowledge and it is worthy of.

I want to say that my father was not mad, nor cruel, nor godless. On the contrary, he was a loving, nice parent. Yes, he had some small obsessions (like the all of us), but I always had bread on my table, clothes, religious instruction and a hug to cheer me up. His sensational death helped people to remind the way he got in touch with the occult and arcane science allowing him to write *Al Azif*; anyway maybe you are living in a country or a time too far from mine and therefore you do not know anything about these facts.

Abdul Alhazred was, since his early childhood, a restless mind, looking for discoveries. He had been single for many years, so that marital duties did not embarrass him in his love for mystery. He travelled a lot. He visited Babylon ruins, Memphis coffins, Irem the Lost, The One Thousand Columns Town. He traversed the red desert, which is called Raba el-khalyeh, exploring its secrets and questioning its enigma, often living alone, for a long period, as required by his mission.

When he was someway satisfied with his knowledge, aged of thirty, Abdul Alhazred decided finally to marry. He married Aisha, my mother, a young widow without children, the daughter of a goat merchant of San'a and in a short time, he had three children, two girls and a boy. The girls were called Kamila and Zahira; and the boy Ismail. From then on, he dedicated to matter-of-fact activities, cattle trading, horse breeding and he didn't think about mysteries and secrets for approx. five years.

One day, while travelling in Arabia's desert with other merchants, he saw some old ruins, and wished to go and visit them.

His travel mates suggested him not to approach the old wrecked village, which had always been here, since the ancestors of their grand-grand-parents of their ancestors first travelled that desert caravan road. In fact, there were bad rumors about this: rumors about buzzing voices, like the ones of invisible insects; rumors about mysterious disappearing, about ghoul eating corpses; about people got mad for unknown reasons or for camping too close to the ruins.

But he has always been a stubborn man and he insisted to go and explore them. So he left the caravan and went hanging out among wrecked walls and old columns, eroded by centuries.

He was very careless, not only stubborn and therefore he got lost very soon, in some moldy crypts, with stale air and full of monstrous statues, strange hieroglyphics, secret frescoes, and mummies of "things" that were not human for sure.

And sometimes they were not completely dead neither.

In fact, after some time, while entering a secret room after another, they started to speak with him.

They had a strange, buzzing voice, going up and down in tone and they told him to come from a planet still unknown to humankind. In their languages, its name was Yoggoth and they explained that it was the last planet turning around the Sun, the farthest, the darkest one and covered in ice, but that they were not born

on that small, very far piece of rock. Yuggoth was only an outpost, a colony. They were from the deep spaces, behind the Milky Way.

Yuggoth inhabitants (calling themselves the Outer Ones), did not look like us at all: they had a shellfish body, they walked upward on feet similar to huge crab claws, they had many limbs, bat wings and an elliptic head, full of small tentacle pyramids, which were their eyes and ears.

They taught their magic and science to my father. They told him that, if he wanted, they would put his brain into a metallic cylinder, through a small surgery, and would take him to visit their planet and other places even more fabulous. In the meantime, the rest of his body would keep on the Earth, ready to take him back, as the body, without brain, doesn't get old.

I don't know the perverse reason why my father accepted this proposal. May be he was tempted right by Iblīs, the Evil Spirit. Or he wanted to emulate our Prophet Muhammad, when receiving during a hermitage the verses of the Holy Qu'rân by Archangel Jibrīl, Abdul Alhazred maybe was thinking to be touched by Allah's grace, willing to let him know more about the nature of things, through this kind of messengers. Yes, I think that he felt as a new

prophet, even if his angels are terrible without being beautiful and his mysteries were deep, without spiritual elevation.

He accepted the proposal of those strange people of Outerspace; he let them put his brain in a cylinder allowing his mind to keep on living, thinking, feeling, seeing, hearing, smelling and remembering; and he left with them towards Yuggoth.

*Al Azif* is not but the poetic transposition of what he saw and learnt during that galactic odyssey.

Yuggoth people instructed him and, finally,

they transported him towards farther and farther spaces, crazier and crazier, the most of them were not following at all any law governing our universe; until they arrived at the Outer Gods', that are the material gods adored and served by Yuggoth people.

Such a travel should take years. But my father's space guides knew how to outdo space and time to their needs. Abdul Alhazred's absence lasted only two months. After that time the Outer Ones wanted to force him to stay with them forever, learning new mysteries and serving their Lord, Yog-Sothoth, Azathoth's vizier.

However, my father backed out of such coercion. He ran away from them in an exciting way and just minded all what he saw and heard; once back to his own body, he came back home. And there he collected all his several notes, completed them with his lively and horrific memories about his mental travel and put them all in written to allow people learning about the true nature of nature, the true history of the world and which are creatures and powers governing the cosmos.

hen he came back home, after three months missing and an endless wandering in desert sands, my father was troubled. He was very slim, his skin was pulled on his cheekbones, he had dark circles, sick complexion and white hair and beard. His eyes looked at you through your body, as if he could see something different from what was visible to others. Looking at him made us trembling.

He did not reply anything to my mother's severe reproaching; not even when she accused him to have spent money for wine and women (which is strictly forbidden by the prophet to good Muslims).

He went upstairs in his study and locked himself in it, asking not to disturb him. And we obeyed without a word, because we were scared by his strange behavior.

When he went out of it, some weeks later, he had written a long poem and that poem was *Al Azif*. He called it like this, because it reported the things he heard from the buzzing voices of Yuggoth people.

Therefore, who declares that *Al Azif* was written in Damascus, is lying or is misinformed. It was wholly written in San 'a, in Yemen, where Dad had always lived. Actually, we moved to Damascus only some months after its writing, because of our neighbors' preconceptions and the persecutions, on the 22nd of Jumâda Al-Awwal, in year 112 from Hegira.

To achieve his work, my father did not sleep, just touched a little food, and he did not almost drink, despite the burning warm of these days. He seemed to me very pale and upset, even sick, and he sent me looking for l'imām Ya 'qūb al-Misrī, because he absolutely wanted to show him the poem and start a theological discussion with him.

I don't know which reaction my father expected, but for sure not the one he obtained. Unfortunately, my father had always been naive and he thought that any man was moved from the need to know the truth, no matter what, as this is the biggest happiness for our race, as for the philosopher from Stagira.

Unluckily, this was only an illusion: the man yearns for comforting lies, not for tiring truth.

While reading *Al Azif* verses, the imām became pale, red, went more and more upset and,

at the end, he started to scream and curse and damn : « You are crazy ! You are a godless ! May Allah throw you in the fire of the Jahannam ! ».
Thereafter, he went out scandalised and scared and we did not see him anymore, except during

Friday preach. And at that time, he shouted at us, among the crowd, arising suspicions and shame on our family.

"Godless" is used to define the ones not believing in Allah and therefore are excluded from Islam. It is not a nice word to say for a Muslim, especially if the object is another Muslim. It's one of the worst accusation you

can receive; the heaviest in terms of conse-
quences.

I knew that my father did not deserve such
a word. He was very devote and God fearing.
Therefore I was hurt and my father even more,
because being considered godless may cost him
not only his honour and reputation, but even
life.

You know how things go: this episode turned
into gossip and in a week all San 'a was repeat-
ing dull imām's version and was whispering
that Abdul Alhazred was mad and godless.

To avoid pranks and general persecutions,
we decided to leave secretly, during the night.

We left the town, shaking the dust down our
sandals, with disdain. We felt victims of injus-
tice and our pride was bleeding; but we, my
family and I, would transform such sorrow in
an armor to be proud of in front of the whole
world, if necessary.

We pointed Damascus, to the North, by cam-
el, because my father had some relatives, in that
far city, and it seemed a place big enough to
start living again as common and anonymous
people. Being anonymous was our biggest desire. And for some time we succeeded in getting
it, even if for few months only.

Then, as I said, the accident of the invisible
monster occurred, and we were forced to run

away from the scandal, the fear and the morbid
curiosity of Damascenes and, most of all, of the
malik of that country, blessed by Allah.

still remember, as if it was today, Abdul Alhazred 's last day of life. Not only because it was the last one, but also because it was admirable, besides tragic. Oblique sunrays were goldening garlic braids hanging on the wall and our house smelt spices, cumin, cloves, pepper and nutmeg. I remember that I opened my eyes suddenly and simply, while my mother and my sisters were still sleeping. I remember that Kamila was snoring and Zahira was lying in a precarious position in the bed.

My father had already got up, at that time, before the roaster crows, and he was cheerful.

«Ismail» he smiled, whispering to ask me not to wake the others up, «Allah sent me a dream.»

«Which dream, my father?» I asked, very excited and expecting big revelations.

«An angel come to me » Abdul told. «I don 't know if he was archangel Jibrīl or another one, but he was a shining and powerful creature. He was not like those others I talked about in my poem : he was frightening but not horrific or driving to despair ; on the contrary he was peaceful. I laid down in fear and did not dare to look at him, being afraid to be burnt by his light. And he spoke, and his voice did not reach my ears, but I felt it in all my body and its substance. And he told : "Abdul Alhazred, Allah, the big, the merciful, made you a witness of deep universe mysteries. Only you, among the mortals, could see the powers governing the universe. You saw the jinn and the demons and learnt about their hierarchies. You were Allah's witness and you served him well, as you wrote all you were revealed with. Now he wants you to pass down your knowledge to someone being able to diffuse it to the most possible illuminated people".

«"To whom ?" I asked, troubled and hesitant.

«"You already know" replied God's angel and disappeared, while I was alone and hesitant in the middle of the big desert. Then I looked into my heart and I knew that it was true : I knew the name of the person going to receive that tremendous gift. As the knowledge is a gift, but also a weight.»

«Who ? Who ?» I asked, while envy was eating me away, of that knowledge heir.

My father smiled and caressed my cheek. His warm and dry palm, slightly smelling oranges and ink, still burns my skin while remembering. «You, Ismail, my beloved child. You'll be my pupil.»

I could not believe my ears. My young mind was full of joy and pride. I was only twelve and I was going to learn about universe mysteries! I was about to scream, being euphoric due

to that unexpected gift, but Abdul closed my
mouth with his hand and told: «Ssh! Neither
your mother nor your sisters should know».

I swore and my father breathed a sigh of
relief. Then my initiation began. «My dear
Ismail, you have to know that Allah did not
make the world from nothing; but the world
was not made wholly for men, his trusted and
perfect servants: even angels had to kneel down
to us. The universe is richer in things and creatures, than we can see.»

«Why, my father?»

«Because our target is witnessing God and
acting according to his will. We are servants in
his palace, but outside the palace, a big number
of invisible creatures moves in the dark. And
they are as necessary to the creation as you and
me. We call them all jinn, without differencing
them, but they are many and all very different
one from another. What are they, actually?
They are material creatures, made up with the
four elements mentioned by alchemists and with
atoms Democritus spoken about, like us. But
you can object that they appear and disappear
like spirits and ghosts, and you are right, Ismail. To understand this mystery, you should
imagine the world as a big sphere floating in
the middle of a bigger sphere, which is floating
in the middle of a bigger one, and so on. The

surface of these spheres is usually impenetrable: but sometimes, when stars are aligned in a specific way, between a sphere and another, a bridge is created. In those rare cases (even if they are not as rare as we would like) and if we are not lucky at all, people from a sphere not belonging to our world can pass through up to us. They appears in our universe and they can be visible and touchable during the star alignment. Only when the astrologic transit is be over, the bridge will break and they will disappear. Did you understand, Ismail?»

I wholeheartedly nodded; but indeed, I had understood very little about my father's speech.

He tenderly smiled and pretended to believe me. «Good boy. Now I'll tell you about jinn's hell hierarchies, in a simple way, so that this complicated subject becomes clear to you and everyone: to simple and sucker men, to laypersons, to godless people, to children... Everyone should be able to understand the truth, if they want to and to be able to use Great Old Ones' science and Outer Ones' doctrine: they are for the ones desiring the truth.

«But before starting our lesson, let's trace a protection circle around us. »he said and drafted on the floor an almost perfect circle, with a two meter diameter and he inscribed in it many curved and curled rays, like stylized tentacles.

« This symbol is Azathoth's seal. While talking about these dangerous subjects, I beg you, Ismail, keep with me inside this circle. Symbols composing it will confuse Outer Gods' strange senses. Actually, should we unluckily pronounce loudly or thinking about an Outer God's name, being under the right star configuration, a bridge could be created and the Outer God could pass through the wall between the worlds. He will be appealed by the sound of his name, or by the glares made by that name

in our minds. He could join us , smelling us.
And then there will be the chance to be... eaten
alive ! Because we are food for those demons
and they did not want our souls, but our bodies' taste ! We are not a need for them, we are
delicacies ! But the curved circle and wavy rays
we traced can deceive them. »

nce entered the magic circle my father had drafted on the floor with a piece or carbon, we sat and Abdul Alhazred started talking about the Outer Gods. «Ismail, where should I start from my lesson? From where, if not from the beginning? As I told you, the universe is a puzzle box, made by concentric spheres, bigger and bigger. However, it is not endless. Beyond the last sphere, there is not more a physical world, but there is the spirits world, where Allah's angels live and where the true believers' souls will go one day. We call that place Jannat.

«But the last sphere of material world, which is the bigger and almost endless, is what we call Jahannam, that is the Hell. And which will be the conditions of people deserving Hell? They will grope in the Samûm and cry in the Hamîm. And they will cough and suffocate, breathing the Yahmûm, which is not cool nor nice. So says the Qur'ân.

« The Outer Gods live there, in that horrible place where laws are upside down. God forgive me, they are Hell's Gods, following Iblīs's laws, the Evil Spirit, the boss of God's angels refusing to kneel in front of man.

« Their caliph's name is Azathoth.

« Azathoth is enormous. So enormous that for him we are invisible. Compared to his size, stars and planets are only dust in the sun. Which is his shape? He does not have a shape. He's the boiling chaos. He's made of fire, of pure energy, of sensing violence. He has a unique aim: destroying, devouring, and absorbing everything. Many stars, whole constellations were devoured by his hunger, in remote times. If he was free, he could swallow the whole universe, sphere after sphere.

« But Azathoth is not free. The demons of his court play shrill flutes and drums and that sound forces him dancing. The caliph is captivated by his servants. As long as they hypnotize him with their eternal concert, he'll be forced by this secret rhythm to keep on dancing, like an enormous sea anemone floating in space waters. Thanks to this dance, the universe cannot end.

Few men could be so fool to summon Azathoth. You will get nothing from him, except for death and destruction. You cannot make any deal with him: he is blind and insensible.

Yuggoth people, however, know a magic spell to call the caliph, the boiling chaos. I wrote it in *Al Azif*, but I do not dare to tell it here loudly, even hidden among the curves of the protection circle.

«Do not summon him, Ismail, never. Never. For no reason. Swear it.»

I swore solemnly and he thanked me with an emotional smile.

bdul Alhazred, my father, sighted before continuing his teaching and dried his forehead from the sweat, as if the memory of the horror he had seen still distressed him, after so many years.

Thanks to this simple move, I noticed for the first time a narrow wrinkle traversing horizontally the upper part of his forehead and disappearing among the hair on the head sides. At a second glance, I understood it was not a wrinkle, but a scar from a surgery, now healed.

«Father, what is this line on your forehead ? » I asked, astonished. How hadn't I noticed it before ?

My father smiled, but his smile was difficult and painful, as if he had eaten a lemon. «Oh, this ! This is the proof I am not mad, even if people say so. You see, Ismail, when I was out for three months (do you remember ?), this was because, during a business trip, I saw from a distance the ruins of a very old nameless village and I went exploring its gloomy cellars. Over there, I met the children of an alien race, looking like monsters, with a buzzing voice, who were in our world, searching for some metals you cannot find in their world, but being very useful or even vital for them. »

He told me about what I already mentioned : the Outer Ones introduced themselves as having a higher level of science and knowledge, than a man could ever dream of. They offered him to put his brain in a metallic cylinder, keeping him alive, to take him with them over the space and the time, to show him the truth about the creation. My father told that he accepted their horrible proposal... for knowledge sake !

« I did not feel any pain » he added immediately, without hiding a tremor. « They inoculated me a strange substance. It was like a scorpion or a snake bite. But it didn 't hurt me. My body was senseless and in such condition, the Outer Ones cut my head and took off my brain. During the operation, I could see everything, but I did not suffer. They put my brain into a cylindrical device, shiny and gray ; but I cannot tell which material it was made of. In the cylinder, there was a transparent substance, like gelatin, and a series of golden threads, that they put into my brain. Thanks to this procedure (but do not ask me how, my son, because

my science is not enough to reply), I could
continue to see, to hear, to smell even being
reduced, to say so, to the essential.

«In this shape, I left with them. A hole was
opened in the crypt ceiling and they flight
through it, flapping their membranous wings.
When we went out through this passage, we
were not under the starry vault of our world,
but in the ice and fire of the deep space, very
close to an iced planet, dark because of its distance from the sun.

«"Look, man of the Earth" said the one
transporting my cylinder. "That bright point
is the star you call the Sun. Now we are at the
border of the Solar System, at almost six bil-
lions kilometers from your birth place."

«I was astonished, amazed and scared. In
my ignorance, I thought that the universe was
really big. Alas, I was just looking at an in-
finitesimal part of the creation and I realized it
very soon.

«"Now, we'll make a stop on Yuggoth"
I was told by the one taking the cylinder,
"because our mission is supplying metals and
rare elements to our scientists. After that, if
you wish, we'll bring you with us, to visit
Cthulhu, Yog-Sothoth and Shub-Niggurath's
lands. They are our gods and, if it is possible
and riskless, you could also admire our supreme

god, Azathoth, who is in the last loop of the universe."

«We went down smoothly towards the white, iced Yuggoth and my mind got lost in following the evolution of the cold dust coming off continuously from the surface of that tiny planet, shining in the eternal night. We reached a strange building, looking like a ziggurat of old Mesopotamian people. But this "Babel tower" was almost as bigger as a mountain and had an obelisk on its top. This obelisk was historiated with hieroglyphics I could not understand. There was an unreal, heavy, threatening silence everywhere. The scarce light and the deep darkness drew clean shadows and fantastic reflexes everywhere, thus giving me the impression to be prisoner of a nightmare.

« Yuggoth people brought me in the ziggurat building and went through a labyrinth in black stone, I've never seen on the Earth. I am not sure, Ismail, but I think it is the same material of the Black Stone, the al-hajar al-aswad, shielded in the Ka'ba, in Mecca, and adored by the idolaters before Muhammad preached Islam (praised and blessed be him).

«I cannot say how much I stayed there. I think for a long time. Months. Years. Yuggoth scientists asked me a thousand questions and replied to all my queries. They told me the story of their race ; explained me the mathematic principles of their science. I was examined, weighted, sounded out with strange tools. Then, one day, some buzzing beings came to inform me that they 'd brought me with them, on a pilgrimage to the sanctuaries of their pitiless and crazy gods.

« In this way, I met the monsters composing caliph Azathoth 's courts. And I 'll describe them to you. But before I need a sip of water »

y father dried off form his beard the water drops caught in it and continued his tale: « The Outer Ones opened a door in the space and time, as they had already done to go over the billions kilometers among the Earth and Yuggoth outposts. They took off in large number, flapping their strange membranous wings, catching star energies and left to achieve their pilgrimage. We flight for a long time in the starry ocean, until we reached a temple, built on the arid moon of a planet near Syrius, in the Ursa Major constellation.

Here, my guides celebrated a ceremony for the honour of the big Cthulhu... »

« Father, who's Cthulhu ? » I asked, while feeling discomforted in my soul.

« He's the high priest of the Outer Gods, and Azathoth is his caliph. Thanks to his science and spells, the Outer Gods can show themselves on the Earth and the Great Old Ones can preserve their corpses while waiting the good star alignment to resuscitate.

« It is a very powerful creature, many cubits high. He looks like a dragon and a turkey; he has a soft belly, like a bladder; his head is like a blind octopus. His eyes are thousands facial tentacles continuously moving. And on his back there are two membranous wings, rather rudimental and not suitable for flying.

« His religion is a bloody one. He requires to his followers human sacrifice and he teaches them many way to hurt and kill. Word ‹ pity ʺ does not exist in his vocabulary.

« He has limitless offspring, almost identical to him, except for height: his children, actually, are never taller than twelve feet.

« Cthulhu's people tried to conquer the Earth, when men were not in Allah's mind yet. At that time, another race come from the space had been governing since eons. They were very clever, having a very sophisticated algebra. They were not animals nor vegetables. They looked like huge cucumbers, walked upright on five " roots " or tentacles and their head seemed a starfish with five points. Their languages was made of musical sounds, similar to flutes and bells.

« The cthulhus attacked with strange blazing weapons. The Great Old Ones reacted, hit-

ting them with their strange weapons, but the chtulhus, even hurt or dismembered, got each time recomposed, and kept on hitting, as if nothing had happened.

«Because of the war, the Great Old Ones were out of luck. The big cucumbers-starfish, little by little, lost their lands and receded in their undersea cities, at Austral Pole. And over there, their civilization fell and got extinguished.

«The big Cthulhu and his children built then the colossal city-mountain of R'lyeh, with wrong corners, where the high priest and his monstrous offspring lived, danced, screamed and killed for many years.

«However, their destiny was not governing our world for an endless time. They reached our world because of the right star alignment, but the big Cthulhu knew that, once the alignment was over, they would die, as they did not belong to this world and without the star magic, they could not survive. Then, the city-moun-

tain R'lyeh, with
wrong corners,
were transformed
in a huge mauso-
leum : the cthulhu
lied down in their
coffins and died at
the right moment.
Anyway, big
Cthulhu's spells
preserved the sub-
stance their bodies
were made of and,
even without mov-

ing or going out of coffins, their minds kept
on thinking ad talking with terrestrial creatures
through dreams, governed by them. « When Allah created men, they talked to the men too and
taught them the basis of their religion. Many
refused such a horrible religion, but some of
them accepted it. That religion kept secret during centuries but its followers keep its rituals
alive and they are waiting the next star alignment to open the Great Old Ones' coffins and
free them.

« In the days of the Flood, R'lyeh sank into
the ocean and disappeared, swallowed by the
shadows and the water interrupted the mental
contact between cthulu thinking corpses and

the followers of that abominable religion. But they have been existing and conveying their forbidden knowledge.

«You can summon the big Cthulhu on Mondays and Fridays, at the new moon. Even dead, he can reply in dreams and will teach to summoning magicians many scientific mysteries, will solve mathematic problems and dissolve philosophic doubts and religious sentences. The spell to summon him should be recited before sleeping, under the effects of a special mushroom (which I'll talk about later) and it is the following:

*Sleeping under the sea,*
*You, big tentacled Cthulhu;*
*dreaming and while dreaming,*

about R'lyeh and among its pinnacles,
whispering telepathic
shadows and terrific worlds
to apathetic human brains,
arise at trine, o Lord!
Arise from the huge sea;
take your reign to men;
burn the remaining
of this man, unaware, shameful.
Big tentacled Cthulhu.

come, prince, I'm summoning you
from the century vastness,
me, your knick-knack, me, your toy.
Under the sea you are sleeping,
Big Cthulhu full of tentacles,
And in your sleep you are dreaming
About R'lyeh and its pinnacles.
And while whispering about a telepathic,
frightening and shadow world
to human brains very apathetic,
arise at trine. oh Lord!

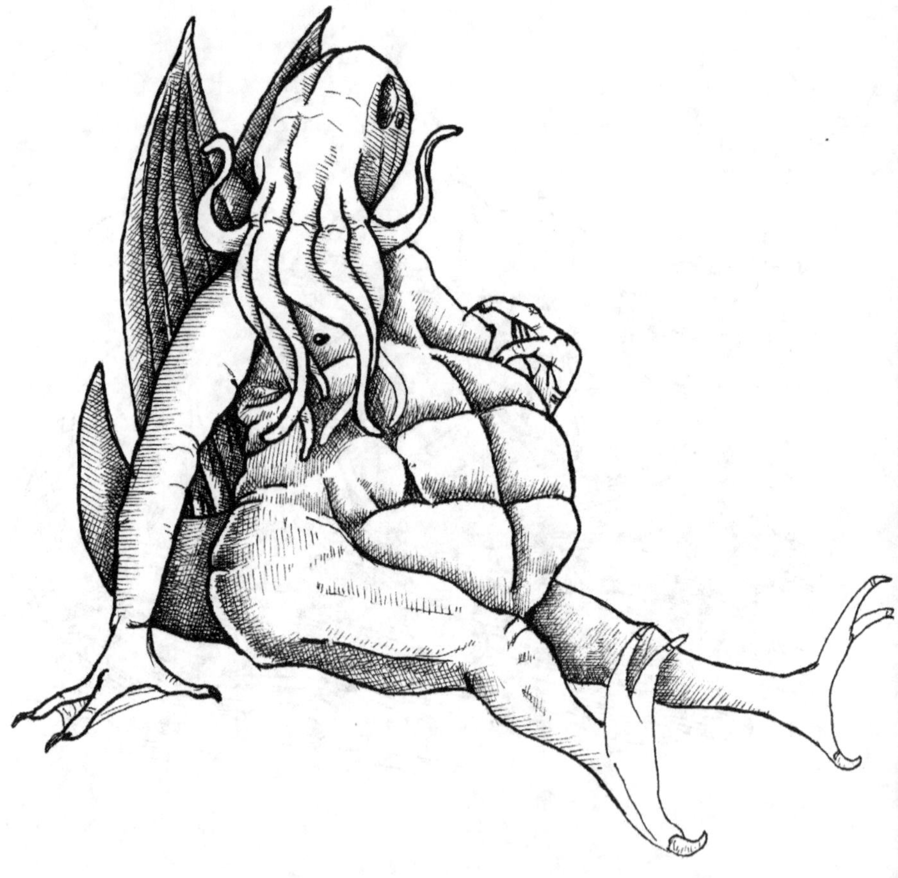

*Arise from the huge sea,*
*Take to humans your reign,*
*It's for me, your devotee,*
*Burn all others, again and again.*
*Big tentacled Cthulhu, his bigness,*
*Come, price, come my boy,*
*From the century vastness*
*I'm your knick-knack, your toy.*

«When you'd like to send away the big
Cthulhu, avoiding his thoughts, Ismail, you
should recite in dreams the following spell:

*Sleep, Cthulu; go back down*
*To your blind, black world,*
*down into dreamless water,*
*under the sea (ring, abyss),*
*into the coffin without*
*light, immobile. And the voluminous*
*in waves and algae, funnel shaded sea*
*be silenced by your horror.*
*So be it, for the good and for the best,*
*while I wake up quickly.»*
*Sleep, Cthulhu, and then go back,*
*To your world which is so black,*
*Down into the dreamless water,*
*Down to abysses, under the sea,*
*Into your coffin, it is lightless,*
*It is black and motionless,*

*And the wavy and algae sea,*
*By your horror silent be.*
*So be it, and for the best*
*While I quickly stop my rest.*

So said my father, Abdul Alhazred.
Blessed be Allah, the biggest, the more merciful.

he nature of things, as explained by my father in a very clear way, opened an abyss in front of my eyes. I suddenly and distressingly felt as if all experiences and rules leading my life so far, were over. To look for a mental support, to cheer me up and hold me out of the arabesque gate of madness, I looked for my mother quiet and unaware face. I was afraid she could surprise me learning forbidden subjects against religion thus blaming me, because of this unholy act.

But, to my great surprise (and a bit of disappointment, I have to say), Aisha was still sleeping and did not seem to be about to wake up. Yet, my father's tale had been lasting for hours, was it possible that such a precise mother and wife was indulging in idleness? I wondered if Abdul Alhazred drugged his family, just to teach me. Such a thought seemed to me monstrous and disloyal, and my father, who seemed able to read my mind, smiled at me with tenderness and fun.

« I did not drug your mother and sisters, Ismail » he said, amused. « This is another lesson for you : inside Azathoth's seal, the time too is different compared to outside. Its curves and angles confuse minutes, hours, years and force them to turn around themselves like dervishes. There, beyond the external circles, time passes as usual ; here, among the isosceles triangles, on the contrary, the time stopped exactly when we sat down and started our lesson. So we have all the time we need, my child, and there is no risk that your mother can surprise you making something she would not approve. »

« Be God blessed, father » I replied, with visible relief.

« Be God blessed, Ismail. Always and in any case » Abdul Alhazred replied.

« What happened after the Outer Ones had made a ritual for Cthulhu ? »

« Cthulhu (I cannot explain how) replied. And he allowed them to continue their pilgrimage, this time to an even further world, to the actual Outer Gods' world. »

« Isn't Cthulhu one of the Outer Gods ? » I asked, puzzled.

« No » my father explained, shaking his head. « He is their " cousin " and high priest ; his uni-

verse is very similar to theirs, but not complete-ly. Cthulhu world is more material than theirs is, which is proven by the fact that he and his people could preserve their bodies when reaching our world. While the Outer Gods, even if they appeared on the Earth, would be invisible to us. It is possible to see them only by blowing al-Ghazi sand over them. But this is not an advantage: seeing them can often kill a unaware person.

«But now let me continue the tale of my extracorporeal peregrinations, my son. As I told you, Cthulhu allowed the Outer Ones to resume their flight towards the heavenly abode of Shub-Niggurath, The Black Goat of the Woods with a Thousand Young, the creature presiding over Outer Gods' orgies. She's also called the wife of the Not-to-be-Named One, that is Yog-Sothoth. Even belonging to the Outer Gods' race, she's rather kinder to men than other entities. She does not only devour and kill, if men are her followers, she gives them sexual bliss and reward the more loyal ones with immortality to have them similar to what Greeks call satyrs. These are horrible and dirty gifts, scaring any devotee amongst Allah's ones, but in any case we must recognize that Shub-Niggurath is demonically favorable to our race.»

«Which is her function, father? I don't understand. And I don't understand why she should protect men whereas her brothers would actually wipe them off the face of the Earth.»

«It's not easy to explain this to a child, Ismail» my father sighed, frowning hesitantly. «She is pure lust and appealed by all creatures reproducing with lust. And among those ones, the man is not second to anybody in the universe... at least until his soul is blocked inside this flesh cage. Shub-Niggurath "loves" sexual creatures, encourages them, increases their hunger and power because she exists to come and make people come. Anyway, it is better not to desire the "happiness" she could give you easily: those are terrible and horrible pleasures, driving you crazy and inhumane. The Outer Gods destroy and there are many way to destroy; not only with pain, but also with pleasure. Finally, Ismail, Shub-Niggurath too would kill you, even if this death seems more appealing.»

«Why is she called The Black Goat of the Woods with a Thousand Young?»

«She's always mating and her children are monsters. They are as black as the ace of spades, made of knobby tentacles. They are approx. twenty feet tall and have a couple of stocky legs. A mass of tentacles sprouts from their trunk, instead of a head. Their sides are covered with wrinkled jaws. These monsters' shape reminds a tree, but they smell an awful stink, like an open coffin. They are the Wood whose Shub-Niggurath is the Goat.

«The Outer Ones are not her favourite, as they have mushroom nature and they reproduce through spores, not mating. They do not know sex pleasures, they are cold, not feeling emotions. Anyway, they worship the Big Mother, as without her approval they could never access the uppermost knowledge of her husband, Yog-Sothoth, who stays next to the Gate, knows the Gate and is the Gate.

« Whereas Shub-Niggurath is the feminine principles of mystic ecstasy, taking the mind beyond itself and the wall of the worlds, Yog-Sothoth is the masculine principle of the organized and organizing science, the guide, the necessary map to understand what will be found in the ecstasy travel. Shub-Niggurath is the sea and Yog-Sothoth the geographer and mathematician, the one determining the course.

« Shub-Niggurath, finally, is the "rhythm" governing caliph Azathoth's dance, and without which the universe would not exist. The blind, mad Outer Gods play their hypnotic music on that rhythm. Shub-Niggurath is the drum and Yog-Sothoth is the flute.

« The Outer Ones led me on a nameless planet, outside the Milky Way, in an unknown space region, orbiting around a double star. Its surface appeared completely covered in dark coloured vegetation. But while approaching the huge temple we were directed to, an unpredictable stench came into my nostrils, as if putrefaction was all around us. And I noticed that it was no vegetation: around the pyramid and the obelisk millions and millions of "Young" were quivering, screaming and

shaking unknown organs, in the throes of fury and rapture.

«It was the most obscene show a mortal can attend, but I learnt something: between desire and death there is a link, called "violence". Where there is violence, there is desire. Where there is death, there is eros. Don't ask why, Ismail. It's one of Allah's mystery and a part of creation enigma.

«The Outer Ones officiated their barbarian

ritual, singing their blasphemous hymns for the Big Mother. And finally, she appeared, curled up on the terrace down the obelisk, lingering, monstrous, full of tentacles, filthy and hypnotic, gigantic, killer, bitch, terrible! »

Abdul Alhazred had to stop. His front was covered with sweat, his breath tumultuous. In his eyes, there was a distressed light, but that was not all: he seemed "excited", too, while thinking about the monster he was describing. Which seemed incomprehensible to me: the words he was using were frightening, but the "tone" was full of lust. Alas, I was too young and naïve to understand, but later I did, oh I did! And I would prefer being still ignorant.

My father closed his eyes and trembled, trying to dominate himself with a big effort. Finally, he succeeded, because he was a religious and godly man and Allah was close to him, but his face was pale and his smile forced. And when he spoke, his voice was hoarse. « You have to summon Shub-Niggurath on Saturdays and Sundays, but also Thursdays, when the moon is full, in the middle of those stone circles arising on woody hills since centuries. In her gracious appearance, she presides over love relationship, she sparks the desire, she makes fertile the infertile couples (however, children born under her influence are often cruel and

evil ) and gives vigour to impotent men. People
seeking for the mystic truth can also turn to her,
as well as farmers facing drought and famine.
She makes imagination fertile, as she does with
bodies; but the works of the poets she "loves",
are always morbid and tremendous.

«You should summon her during the sex, otherwise it will be useless:

*Come, come, Big Mother,*
*Goat with black young,*
*you, Shub-Niggurath, milady,*
*you, arousing spasms,*
*you, instilling lust.*
*Come, come and visit your slave;*
*give your terrible gifts*
*to your uncontrolled slave*
*who blasphemes against each chain.*

«To exorcise her, on the other hand, you
have to read this spell out, pressing your testi-
cles with strength:

*The drum falls silent,*
*The excited heart falls silent.*
*Now leave me in peace;*
*let me take a breathe;*
*let my blood powerless.*
*Be the erotic caves*

*weak, empty, sterile;*
*and your cosmic womb*
*be closed. The seismic*
*drum falls silent. I am dry*
*and a sinner in front of you,*
*among your ignoble young. »*
*The drum falls silent now*
*And the excited heart too,*
*Leave me in peace, wow !*
*Let me take a breathe for true;*
*And be my blood without waves.*
*Be all the erotic caves*
*weak, empty, sterile;*
*Be closed your cosmic womb*
*silence the seismic drum,*
*I am dry and arid too,*
*and a sinner in front of you,*
*among your young full of evil.*

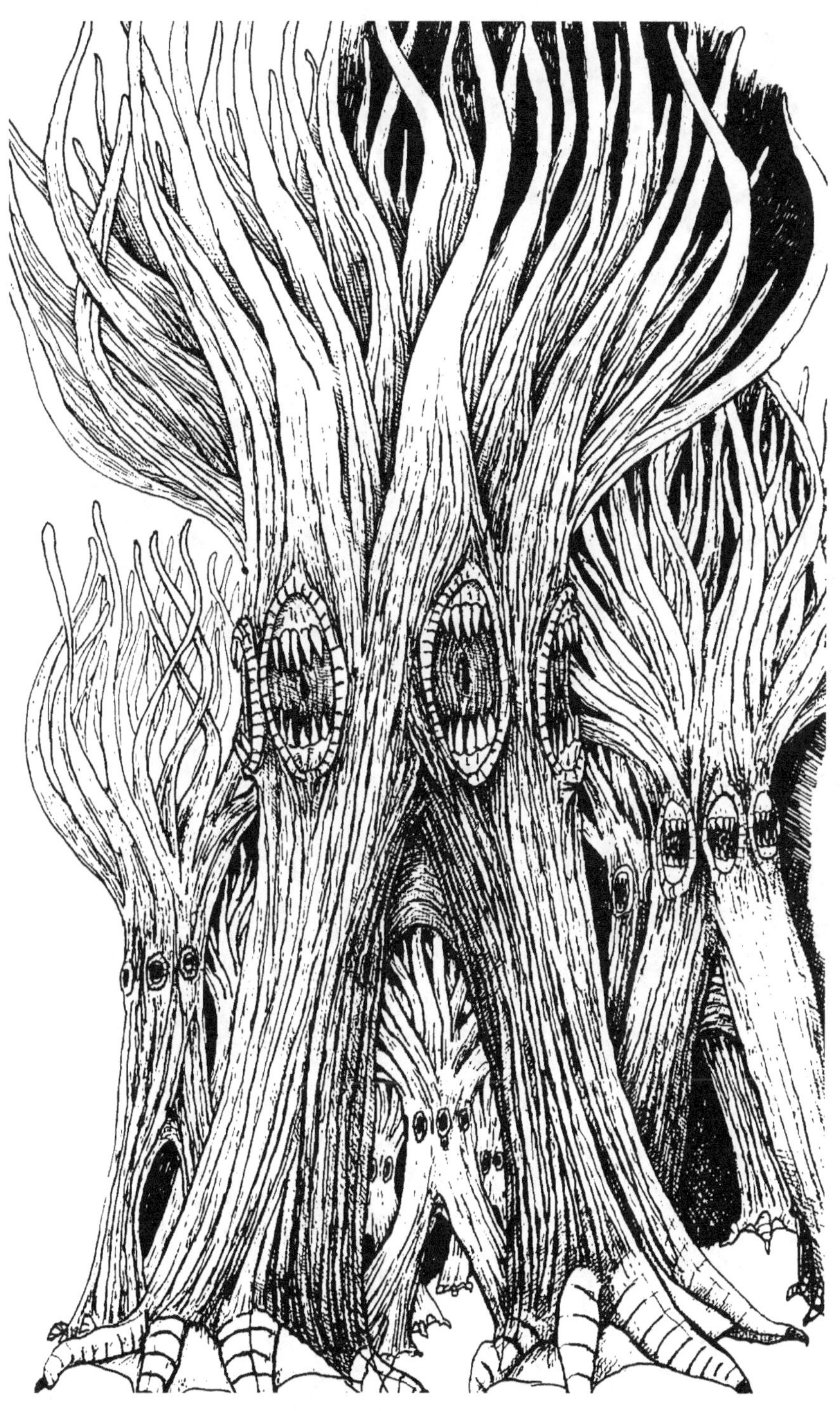

eaving from Shub-Niggurath's vague and unreal tentacles was a relief, but a relief going to change into further horror and distress, because the Outer Ones were about to reach Yog-Sothoth's, Outer Gods' vizier, sanctuary. My father's tale had been leading me definitely away from normality, peace and serenity.

« You have to know, Ismail, that for unaware people, religion and magic are easy to be mixed up. However, a superficial glance drives them into this guilty mistake. In fact, the religious man puts his efforts to avoid demons and jinn to pass the gate between worlds, while the magician puts his efforts to summon those same demons and jinn, because he hopes to be able to dominate and use them for his purposes. Alas, this is impossible : Allah made the sphere walls using religious and devote men's prayers, to protect his best but most fragile servant. Breaking or even chipping that mystic barrier is insane. Magic, Ismail, is like a fixation, a mental illness, a misunderstood and aberrant type of spirituality. People dealing with magic are unfailingly evil, but also "stupid", victims of their own fetishes (by blindness, incontinence or lack of faith in true God). A good spirituality aims to the elevation of the physical substance towards transcendence, while magic aims to the opposite: it does not send anyone Above: it has the absurd and tragic presumption (assuming risk and responsibility) to summon the Above in the physical world. Magic has "operators", but not "heroes" nor "champions". It inverses the process, perverting it. But container and contents cannot exchange their roles, no matter how much time and energy you spend.

«I'm telling you so, because I want you to know against what you have to fight in the future. Million years ago, men did not exist, but the Outer Gods, the Old Ones and Cthulu (their high priest) did. Men did not exist and then there it was no barrier between our world and other demoniac ones: as you already know, the Earth too was governed by monsters. But Allah closed the gate and the jinn were obliged either to "die" or to go away. This made the monsters furious and inspired their centuries-old revenge willing.

« And that's not all, my child. Before being sent away, the thinking cthulhu corpses and Cthulhu's one in particular, " spoke " to some men and taught them Outer Gods' secret religion. »

« I know, father, you already told me... »

« Ismail, then let me repeat, because, if you do not understand this point, all my teaching will be useless. I received a revelation and I wrote *Al Azif*; but I am not the first one to know universe monstrous secrets. Thousands year before me, others learnt them and perpetuate them, in secret. These jinn followers does not want the truth to be told to anyone. All those who tried to, were killed. Now I told everyone the truth and they will try to kill me. And they'll try to kill you, too, my dearest son. Be careful, always ! »

I quivered, but promised to be careful, so that Abdul Alhazred became calmer and continued his tale.

« The Outer Ones left, therefore, towards Yog-Sothoth. The universe as we know it had disappeared and the space around us, was distorted and full of " things " I cannot describe : unknown geometrical shapes, creatures and objects coloured outside the visible optical spectrum and its mixing...

« Were we still going on ? My mind could not

understand the space nor the time in that messy universe. I could guess we were still travelling, however I could not sense it.

«"Man of the Earth" told me the one taking the cylinder I was in, "we are arriving very soon at the Not-to-be-Named One's, at Outer Gods' vizier's, at the one whose power is second only to Azathoth's one, at Yog-Sothoth's. Maybe your brain will be driven crazy, looking at him, as he is beyond a small brain like yours. If you survive, however, your evolution may have a big increase. Yog-Sothoth is the owner of the four alchemic elements and he has the power to change the ones into the others and to mix them according to his will. He's the only owner of any substance, especially organic and living one. No matter which alchemist is devoted to him, while involved in the Big Work, aiming to transform the man in something more."

«Then he did not speak any longer and his buzzing voice turned off. The travel carried on, but the strange and unclassified objects of that universe were not "coming towards us", as it usually happens when moving forward. They were only changing, turning on and off, continuously muting. This rhythmic transformation, failed to paralyse my brain capacities and I did an effort to keep my self-control.

«So far, I've been feeling protected in my

partners' "hands", even safe, but in that moment (who knows why), in that crazy world light, I suddenly realised my complete powerlessness. In fact, I could not move, defend myself and, most of all, go back to my body. I felt instinctively that there is another way, simpler and less risky, to make the travel I was making, not requiring any surgery or material shifting: through the dreams.

«When we dream, Ismail, our soul travels and is free to pass through the barriers among the worlds, as it is transcendent and intangible and only Allah has power on it. On the other hands, all the demons I had seen and would see later, were physical creatures, made of strange energies and very strange atoms, but they did not have any power on my soul, even if they were strong and terrible.

«I understood they had cheated me and I was taken by a cold and endless fear. What could I do if the Outer Ones did not want to put my brain at its place, inside Allah's tabernacle, my body? Nothing. I'd never be able to force them.

«And after doubting and fearing, an awful certainty made its way in me: they would not do it. They had cheated me. They had separated my brain from my body to prevent my escaping through the only way they had no power on : my soul. The soul is everywhere inside the body, in brain too, and it is in any part of us, even if this part is kilometers far away). So mine could not run away to my complete body, because my body, or better, two parts of it, were in two different places at the same time !

«My child, I am not able to tell you how distressed I was in that moment of extreme clarity. The Outer Ones had appealed me with the promise of upsetting revelations, but they had no good intentions. Their secret aims were to use me for their purposes, not to give advantages to me. I had been a fool.

«"Man of the Earth" buzzed the one taking the cylinder I was closed in, like the jinn in the fisherman's bottle, "the device you are in measures your thoughts, through elements and fluids they create in your brain. If well read, these data result in a sort of mind reading. We know what you are thinking about. I can see you are scared and you finally understood your situation, partially. As you are in our hands and you cannot escape, we can stop the pretense. Yes, we cheated you. The aim of our purpose is not letting you tell other men about things that, on the contrary, have to be kept secret. We have revealed to you some mysteries just to better cheat you and to distract you from what was clear since the beginning. The purpose of our travel is taking you to the big Yog-Sothoth, the vizier, the owner of the substances, so that he can use you for his alchemic permutation experiments. He tried many times to reach the Earth, both directly, and by generating with mortal women some hybrids that could survive in your existence level, but without success. Now, we are going to make him a big and rare service: we are taking him a human sample... even if reduced to the essential. We are taking it to him, in his existence level, where he's stronger and we are doing so that it cannot be called back to its world, like it would happen if it was complete."

«"What will become of me?" I asked, frozen, unable to think.

«"Yog-Sothoth will make you evolve, he will change you into a being more than human, better, able to survive and exist both on his and his own existence level. And he will make use of you (when you'll be enough powerful) to destroy the human race, as well as other disgusting forms of life on Earth. In this way, the mystic barriers will fall and the Earth will go back to the abyss from where it was saved by Allah's will."

«A terrible destiny was expecting me and I begged Allah's pardon for my vainglory and my knowledge greed. »

y father suddenly stopped his tale and as he seemed unable to continue, being too distressed by his adventure memory. I finally asked: «My father, how could you run away from demons' claws? How could you convince the Outer Ones to take you back here?».

This question stirred him from the cesspool of his horrors and he started again to talk.

«At the beginning, I could not find any solutions and gave up. I thought that I could only wait for my sad destiny and God's will being done. But, while giving up so cowardly, I went back to the magnificence I had heard, seen, learnt and to the unbelievable principles handed down to me by the Outer Ones. And, incidentally, I remaindered a story they told me. Million years after the extinction of the Old Ones and cthulhu on Earth, our planet gave birth to another evolved race. They seemed wrinkled cones, with tentacle appendixes on the top and they knew many mysteries. The biggest one, that they looked after very carefully and characterizing them most of all, was the capability to throw their consciousness in others' bodies. When they decided to do it (usually for study reasons, as they were very good scientists), between the wrinkled cone and the other creature, there was a sort of exchange. Cone's mind entered temporary host's body and host's mind entered temporary cone's body.

«Of course, this was not a riskless operation and often there were accidents. If during the exchange the cone's body died, his mind would remain forever in host's body. But it had also some advantages: all races are going to extinguish. But this Big Race could throw his members' souls into past or future creatures and find out the exact time and reasons of extinction. They could also avoid it, going all together into others' bodies. In this way, their bodies would have died, but souls inside those bodies would have been of a different race. By this ruse, the Big Race had escaped death many times, to the detriment of innocent creatures.

«While brooding all these histories, I remembered also that the Outer Ones had discovered the Big Race's secret, extorting it from one of their scientists, "visiting" a body of a member

of Yuggoth's people. They recognized him by his strange behaviour, different and ignorant about habits and customs of the Outer Ones. The intruder was skillfully tortured and had to admit everything. I don't want to talk about this, Ismail, but Outer Ones' methods can be very convincing and I wouldn't wish any enemy to fall into their hands.

«In any case, there was a spell to start the exchange they told me about carelessly, while I was still in the ziggurat on Yuggoth. Hope came back to me suddenly. If I could remind the spell and the relevant ritual, maybe I could escape. But I had to wait for the right moment, and the success was not granted, as my human mind was not similar to the Big Race's one.

«While brooding, I saw on the horizon (in front of me, in that chaos of transformations) terrible vizier Yog-Sothoth's shape. And nearly I fainted!

«Yog-Sothoth was a huge and diffused creature! His body seemed composed by many bodies, connected at a distance to incomprehensible and invisible powers. He was a constellation of translucent and changing buboes, pounding obscenely. Each substance island composing his shapeless shape was full of eyes, antennas, tentacles, pincers, limbs, tails...»

Abdul Alhazred stopped again, covering his

eyes with his hand and trembling, fighting against himself and his tremendous memories. «That melting pot of putrefying substance (but still shining, like soap bubbles and foam), smelling bad, that cancer ready to explode and whose metastasis filled in the space... it was what the Outer Ones called Yog-Sothoth!

«And behind the chaotic, excessive, incomprehensible aspect, you could guess a semi-di-

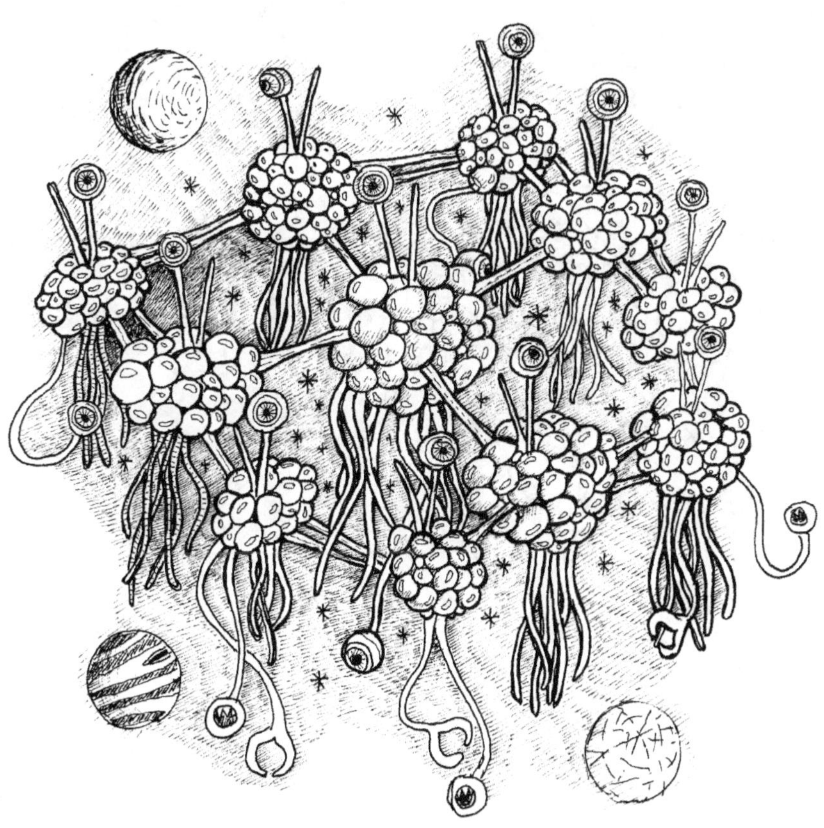

vine strength and intelligence. I beg Allah's pardon, I am cursing: that frightening creature was what is closer to God's idea in this material universe.»

Upon hearing this blasphemy, I naturally touched wood.

«For an endless moment I was overwhelmed by what I saw and sensed. I felt, in fact, a creeping, unwavering and evil will, catching me little by little. It was seizing my weak con-

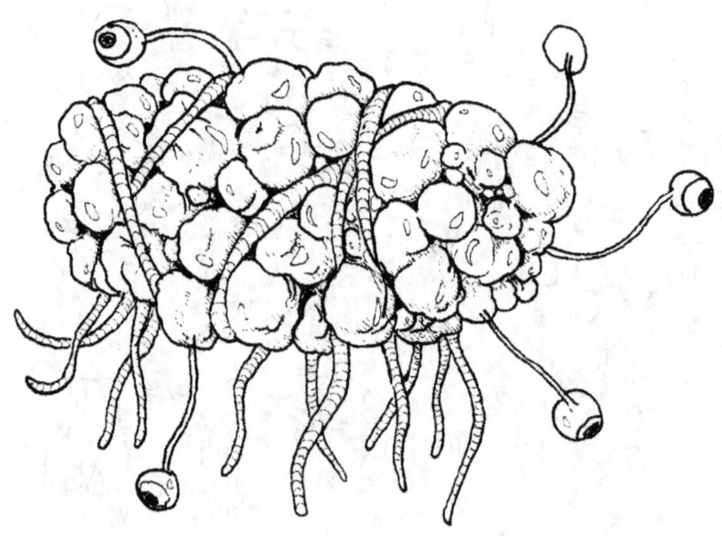

sciousness, surrounding it by its waves, scanning it, testing it and trying to dissect it.

«I understood that I had to react immediately, before huge and alien Yog-Sothoth came too close to me. I felt that if he had only touched me physically, I'd go lost. Therefore, with a big effort, I drove away the groping, ranting, fear looming over my soul and I mentally repeated the change spell, trying to throw my id in the repulsing body of the one taking my metallic cylinder.

*I am me. Who are you?*
*I will be and I was. You will be.*
*I am me and we are us.*
*I am you and you are not.*
*You are me and I am you.*
*According to Yog-Sothoth's law!*

«After the spell, nothing happened for a while. Yog-Sothoth was closer and closer. My mental health was more and more waving and I was afraid that the magic wouldn't work.

«But then I realised something was changing, very slightly. My vision was fading, muting. I did not see the shapes as I did before, but as tangles of pulsing and floating energies. Everything was more confused but also clearer.

«I tried to direct my glance and it fell on the

metallic cylinder... I was looking at it from the outside! I did it! My mind was in the Outer One's body.

«I examined the possibilities I had. I was not sure to be able to control it, but first Yog-Sothoth's ramifications were too close to me and it was almost too late for me. I had no time to delay my escape.

«Then, I tried to move one of the six upper limbs of my host, looking for the portable
device used by the Outer Ones to jump in the
space and among the dimensions and pushed
blindly the stud in soft material, turning it on,
without regulating it before. It was crazy. But
it also saved me: as I dit not select any destina-
tion, any pursuer could not find me.

«In the apparently empty space cloth, a hole
opened and I plunged into it, flying very fast
and strongly, before Yuggoth's people could
understand what happened.

«And so I escaped from my terrible destiny,
Ismail.»

was scared and astonished. The amazing things my father had told me, had completely distressed my heart but, at the same time, they had opened in front of me unbelievable scenarios. "The world" I thought, "is really big and wonderful. Blessed be Allah"

Anyway, I was happy about the history ending, because it was difficult for me thinking about my father in such big horrors.

But Abdul Alhazred deceived me immediately. «I was rescued from the immediate danger, represented by Yog-Sothoth... to go from pillar to post. I did not know at all where I was. I had no point of reference, and I was trapped in a disgusting body whose senses and mechanisms were unknown to me and refused by my mind as an abomination. Can you imagine the fear I felt, my child ? »

I shacked my head, unable to pronounce a single syllable.

« Well. Nobody, I think, will ever feel it. Or at least, I hope.

« In any case, Allah led my thoughts and I remembered that the device allowing me to get free, had a sort of sextant. If I could regulate the jump on a point of reference, I'd be able to come home.

« On the device, there were symbols and numbers I could not understand, as the Outer Ones use a foreign alphabet, completely different from the Arab, Greek or any terrestrial alphabet. Therefore, this was not a possibility for me.

« But those small tools, my child, are unbelievable pieces of art. They have a small artificial brain, with big memory. They were, in fact, able to "remember" all the travels they did in a chronological order. I just had to turn a wheel and on its transparent surface, I could immediately see some symbols looking like stylized maps and diagrams representing itineraries. I found easily the one taking me back on the Earth.

« Unfortunately, my happiness did not last long. I said I did not know where I was. Well, I discovered it immediately. And I would have discovered it even before, if my new senses were not so unknown to me, to block my mind.

There was something strange in the place I

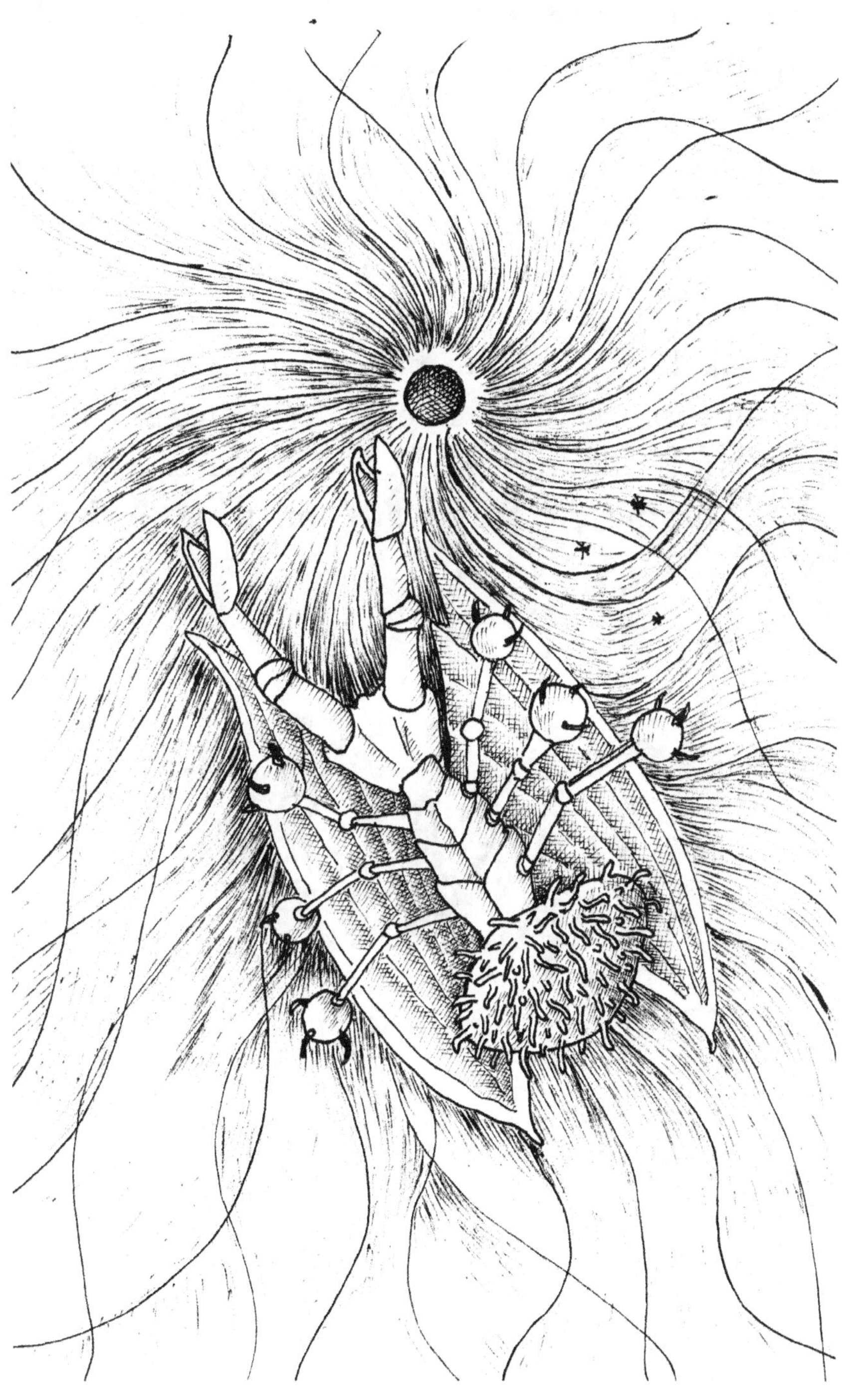

was after my escape; something I could not explain, but scaring me.

«The space was completely empty. Or rather, almost completely "full" of something I mistook for a tangle of stars. My physical distress was coming from there. But what was it, finally?

«I made an effort to better watch, even if I did not see like men. I could see thousands and thousands stars, shining like furnaces... they were shining but they were not stable in their

places or around their orbits. They seemed to arrange in very long floating lines, moving at the same time, as if they were connected each other. The whole of these several lines was continuously moving. In general, they seemed to be dancing, following an inaudible rhythm.

« I could not understand. Those huge, endless " star tentacles " seemed useless, but they were appealing and charming me. Each atom of the body I was occupying was vibrating together with those incomprehensible stars' cosmic dance. It was shaking to cut the links forcing it so have the shape of a sensitive mushroom, to get free, to reach that tangle or rotating stars, having in its middle an orange fire ring, with a dark hole in its centre...

« Finally, I got it: I was in the true heart of Hell and I was looking to Azathoth in person, the Outer Gods' caliph, the creature that, if free, would devour the universe! The long dancing star lines were his energy tentacles, moving eternally in the total emptiness and the fire ring in the middle was not but his mouth.

« And he was getting closer! He was coming to absorb in his non-shape, the only piece of substance in his hunting ground, after swallowing all that was there, including time, space and light.

« I was terrified.

«It was not Azathoth coming closer. He's immobile in the centre of the universe, its dark navel. It was me, unintentionally, not being able to prevent it, going closer to him!

«And, so doing, I was crumbling in dust and lapilli! My atoms architecture was about to collapse.

«I pushed immediately the device soft spud and I ran away just in time.»

So said Abdul Alhazred.

smail, I saw and experienced the maximum horror. But I think I would not be here, sane, if I had lived those experiences through my human senses. I could get out of it just because I was in a different body, whose structure and senses were made of superhuman material, suitable for difficult open space conditions. You know, over there; there is no air, no warm, only destroying energy. Those senses and substance are very precise but unable to discern their emotions and feelings.

«I reached immediately an universe similar to ours and I stayed there the necessary time to recover and thinking.

«I had escaped from my kidnappers and Azathoth's destruction, but how could go again into my body, once come back on the Earth? In the nameless village, I'd found Abdul Alhazred's remains... alas together with a dozen of mushrooms-shellfish! I would never be able to deceive them, they were too diabolic and astute. They are not afraid about killing a member of their own race, as they do not know neither filial nor fraternal love. Guessing the danger, they would kill the body I was occupying, without hesitating.

«Putting my brain into my body was quite simple: I just had to put the cylinder it was in close to the open head and then push a handle. The cylinder would make it by itself. Then I just had to close my head and weld it with a special blue light, created by the Outer Ones to heal their hurt soldiers during battles. But after the operation, I would have to rest, defenseless. So, if I did it in the presence of the Outer Ones, I could not remain alive all the same.

«No, I had no choice. My only possibility was surprising them. I had a weapon (as all the Outer Ones), a wand able to cast a killer light. I had to jump on the Earth and slaughter aliens... before they slaughtered me.

«I pried Allah to make me win, then I pushed again the soft spud and jumped down to our world, to the nameless village I had left from.

«I was greeted by a mold, curdled milk and lobster smell, issued by the Outer Ones' bodies.

«My sudden arrival wreaked havoc among Yuggoth's diabolic scientists. I flew among them, through the piece full of flickering and vibrating machines, and mowed down, in my flight, at least three mushrooms-shellfish, crashing carapaces and cutting a head full of disgusting appendices. But then I crashed against a mysterious equipment, breaking one of my membranous wings.

«I was traversed by a sharp pain, but I ignored it. It was not my body and I was too worried about failing. Then I immediately took my weapon-wand and started to cast flashes of killing light, piercing three Outerspace creatures' armors and reducing other heads to a gray and lumpy mash, made of yellowish ichor.

«I am not a warrior, Ismail, and I am not good in telling actions scenes...

«The two mushrooms-shellfish still upright tried to react but they were too slow and shy, luckily, so I massacred them before they could cast their killing light.

«Only at that moment I felt the pain of my broken wing and I understood that it was a moral wound and that small time had remained to do what I had to do. I took the cylinder containing my human brain. During the battle, it had fallen and rolled over a corner. I prayed it was not damaged, otherwise all would have been useless, but it seems that those objects are very solid and the cylinder was in a proper condition.

«Then I get closer to the wood and glass coffin, containing my dear, old human body. That strange coffin (looking like the shrines used by the heretic Christians to preserve their saints' remains) contained Abdul Alhazred's mortal remains, keeping them alive through flexible straws going in and out every orifice. In this way, the heart was keeping on beating, the lungs breathing and each organ working, taking liquid food to the stomach and collecting faeces and urine in some poches, looking like fish bladders.

«Despite any opinion we may have on the Outer Ones, we cannot but recognize that they are first-rate scientists.

«I toddled goofily towards the coffin and I opened it, despite the pain I felt each move. I opened the head of my poor inanimate body and put the cylinder next to it, pulling the ejecting gray handle.

«The operation lasted two minutes. The mushrooms-shellfish's machines worked well: my brain went back to its place, an articulated metallic silver arm welded the cut nerves with the healing blue light, another one closed the head and welded the bones. After, one by one, the flexible straws got out from Abdul Alhazred's flesh. A last arm inoculated a greenish substance into his heart.

«At that moment, my body suddenly wide opened my eyes and started to move in a convulsive way, as it was occupied by a guest having no familiarity with it. I was impressed by the evil and idiot expression on my face (I had difficulties in recognizing me, as none of the facial expressions I was seeing belonged to me) and the powerless, inhuman, hate glance I saw in my eyes.

«The body I was occupying was about to die, but I did not know how much time this would take. As longer as there was life in it, it was dangerous for my human body safety. Then I did a last thing, before reading out the exchange spell: I dragged the Outerspace carcass

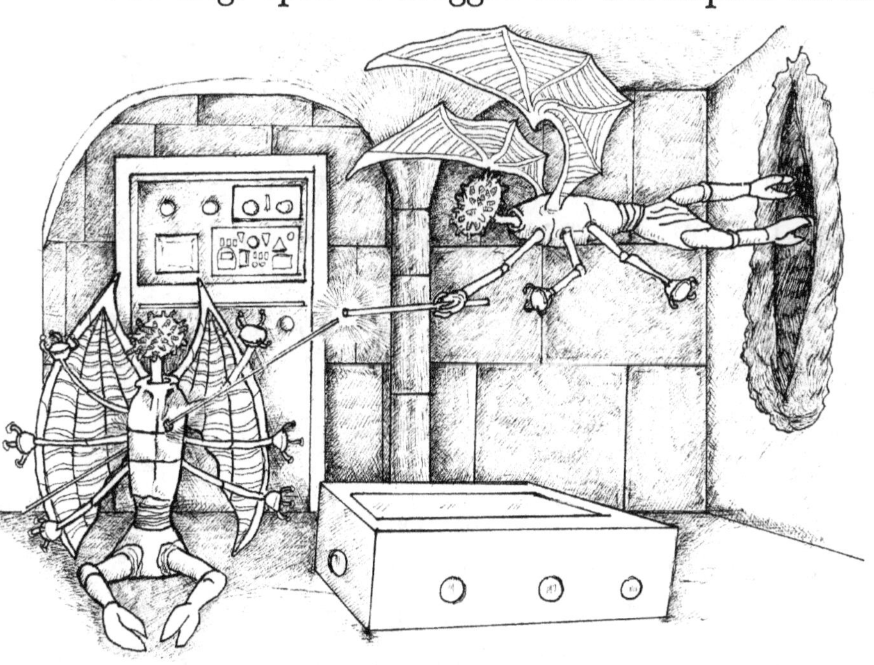

in a small piece, locked the door, destroyed the lock with a flash of the killing light and finally I break the weapon-wand so that it could not be used any longer.

«Only then I read out the spell and went back to my head. I felt a pain, as if ten thousand needles were piercing my skin at the same time. I would had to wait for the pain to decrease, but I was too afraid that the Outer Ones were about to find me. Therefore I rolled about and slithered as quickly as I could along the endless aisles, the smelling dark crypts of the nameless village, panting for the effort of my contracted muscles and moaning by pain and fear.

«And when finally I reached the surface and my face was kissed by the noon sun, and my knees went down into the soft and warm sand, I cried a disrupted blessing to Allah.

«I don't want to tell you about the pains I suffered, Ismail, because I was so happy to be home again, that I did not even felt them. I had no food, nor water and I was in the middle of the desert, but I did not care about dying, because I could die as a man, in my body, which I was created in to live and die. I knew that I was going to die, but Allah (all blessings be to him) wanted to help me and the fourth day, while toddling thirsty, hungry, burnt by the warm, suffering terrible headaches and fe-

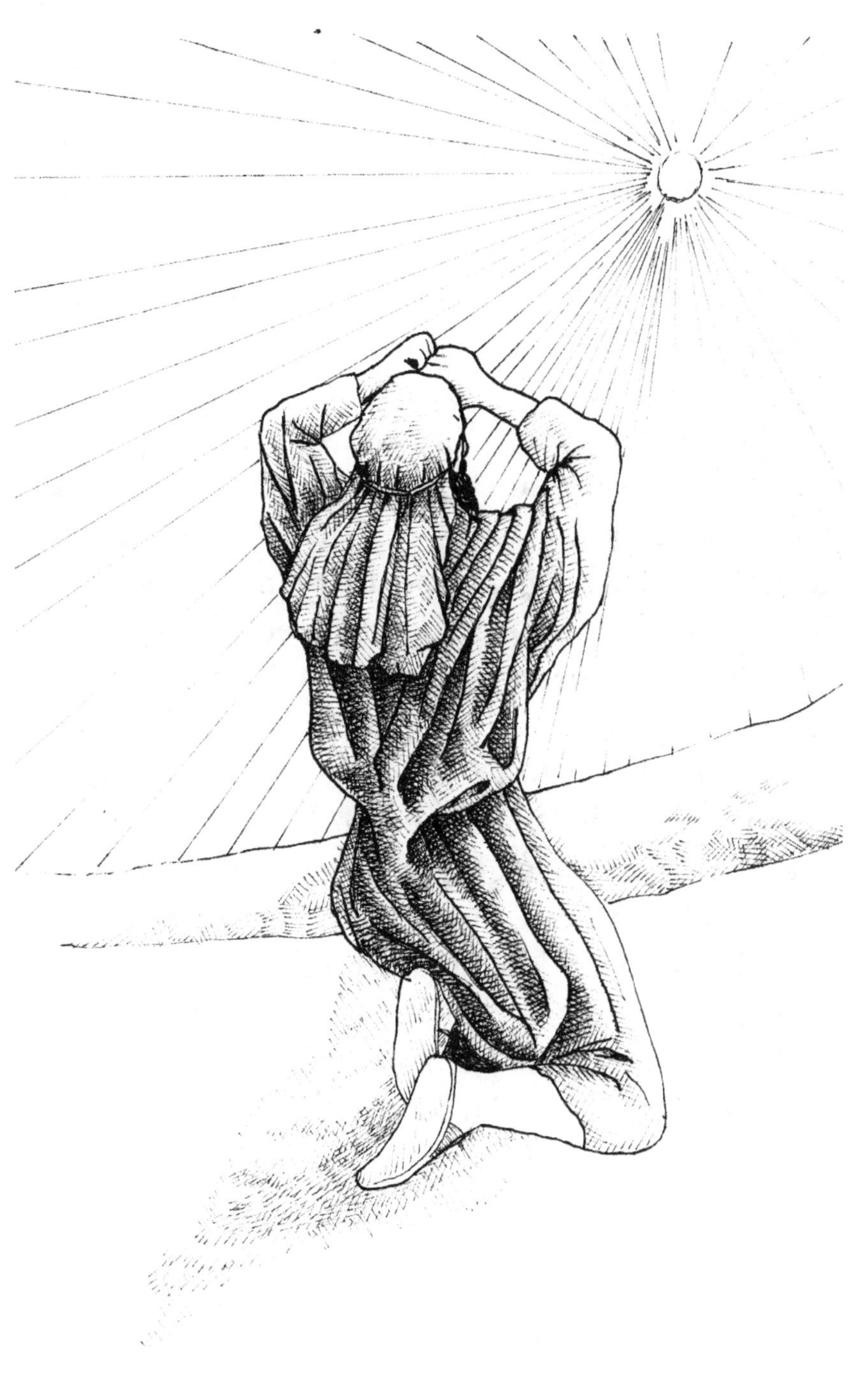

ver, he sent a merchants' caravan to cross my unstable steps.

«I was picked up and healed by those godly men and they took me with them, bearing my frightening delirium.

«Once recovered, I came back to San 'a, with you, and I wrote what was to be written for God's people to be informed about the big danger continuously threatening them and doubled their efforts to be pious and worshipper. Prayers, faith and alms, my dear Ismail, are an actual bulwark against space demons and jinn and strengthen the barriers between the worlds. God's work survival until the Day of Judgement's depends on them. Remember, we are the butlers of the castle, we have to preserve God's town, which is the whole world. And one day we will have to welcome our Lord, and give him back the keys, undergoing to his exam. If we give him back a ravaged garden or, worse, if we could not welcome him because we did not guard and marauders went in and killed us, how will we be judged by our Creator?

listened to the end of my father's odyssey, he told me with beautiful poetic skills, and I had tears in my eyes, due to his terrible sufferings and his unbelievable bravery. No child could be more pride than I was of his father. His escaping from such a painful situation, spoiling jinn's aims was a miracle to me.

«Before the end of this long preliminary lesson comes, Ismail, my beloved child, I wish to tell you about a last demon race. You already know about the Outer Gods, the Cthulhu, the Old Ones, the Great Race and the Outer Ones. Well, there is another race, I did not talk about in this story: the Deep Ones. The Deep Ones are not Outerspace creatures. They are Terrestrials like the Great Race. All come from Dagon, they worship as a God and live under the sea. They look like "human" fish and breathe water through gills. Their back is gray and covered with scales but their bellies and limbs are smooth and greenish. They have fish face and protruding eyes, without eyelids. They can walk on the mainland and breathe the same air we breathe, for a while. This is why I think and I don 't believe I am wrong, that they are amphibious like frogs and like frogs they have long palm-like fingers.

«Under the whole world waters, they built cities, and the oldest, the most famous and the biggest is Y 'ha-nthlei. It is said to have at least one thousand hundred years, but, from some discussions I had some times ago with the Deep Ones, I am likely to think that it is much older.

«These amphibious creatures are more or less immortal, except for violent death, and, unlikely us, never stop growing up.

«But the most disturbing thing that was revealed to me, is this : the Deep Ones mate in secret with human beings thus generating abominable hybrids. Those hybrids spend the first part of their life on mainland, mingled with men. But when they grow up, they start having visible monstrous features : ears disappear, eyes protrude and loose eyelids, gills appear at the neck sides, the head becomes smaller and hairless, the skin starts being covered with scales...

«When they become adults, they cannot hide anymore, as their aspect is too visible and they move living under the sea, where they serve their father Dagon and celebrate his rituals.

«Dagon is a creature similar to Cthulhu, even if more "terrestrial". He looks like an enormous, very ugly fish. He smells very badly, worse than any fish shop. Like all other Old Ones he's huge, much bigger than a sperm whale, but less than Cthulhu.

«You can summon him on odd days of pair

months and when the new moon is on Friday. He gives his followers rich and copious fishing, and he gives them the treasures found in sunken boats. In exchange, he wants his children to mate with human beings. To make a deal with him, therefore, you need to have a sister or a brother ready to marry a Deep One.

« The spell to summon Dagon is the following and has to be read out naked, on the seaside, between one and three am:

*Under the green waves and floats,*
*Dagon, prince of fish,*
*you have been increasing, growing for centuries.*
*Tell me, how many men have you destroyed,*
*and how many sailors have you devoured?*
*Drowned men's dumb voices*
*Have already wished you evil.*
*Come, erupt from your whirlpool.*
*Sign the deal I am proposing you.*
*Under the waves and floats of the green sea,*
*Prince of fish, mighty Dagon,*
*always growing up, carrying on,*
*how many men have you killed, tell me,*
*haw many sailors have you devoured, I want to see!*
*Drowned men's dumb voices*
*Are wishing you evil, didn't you notice?*
*Come, erupt from your whirlpool,*
*Sign my deal, it is so cool!*

« And the one to send him back :

*Dagon, Dagon, sleep, go down,*
*In the mass of dirty water.*
*Go back to the green sea,*
*into the abyss, in the salt.*
*Appease your hunger and giant sharks,*
*sperm whales and squids,*
*eat, instead of*
*the one reciting prayers.*
*Sleep Dagon, and go down, filthy,*
*In the mass of water, dirty.*
*Go down back to the green sea,*
*In the abyss and salt be !*
*With sharks, appease your hunger,*
*With sperm whales, old squid or younger,*
*Eat them all in many layers*
*And not me, telling the prayers.*

« Ismail, here you are. That's all. Now you know the truth about your father. The one knowing his father, knows himself and can do anything he wants : the whole world is his, as he is free in the world. My first lesson is over. We'll have time, if God wants so, to tell you which other beings I was allowed to know and study. Now let's go out from the magic circles and go back to our usual life »

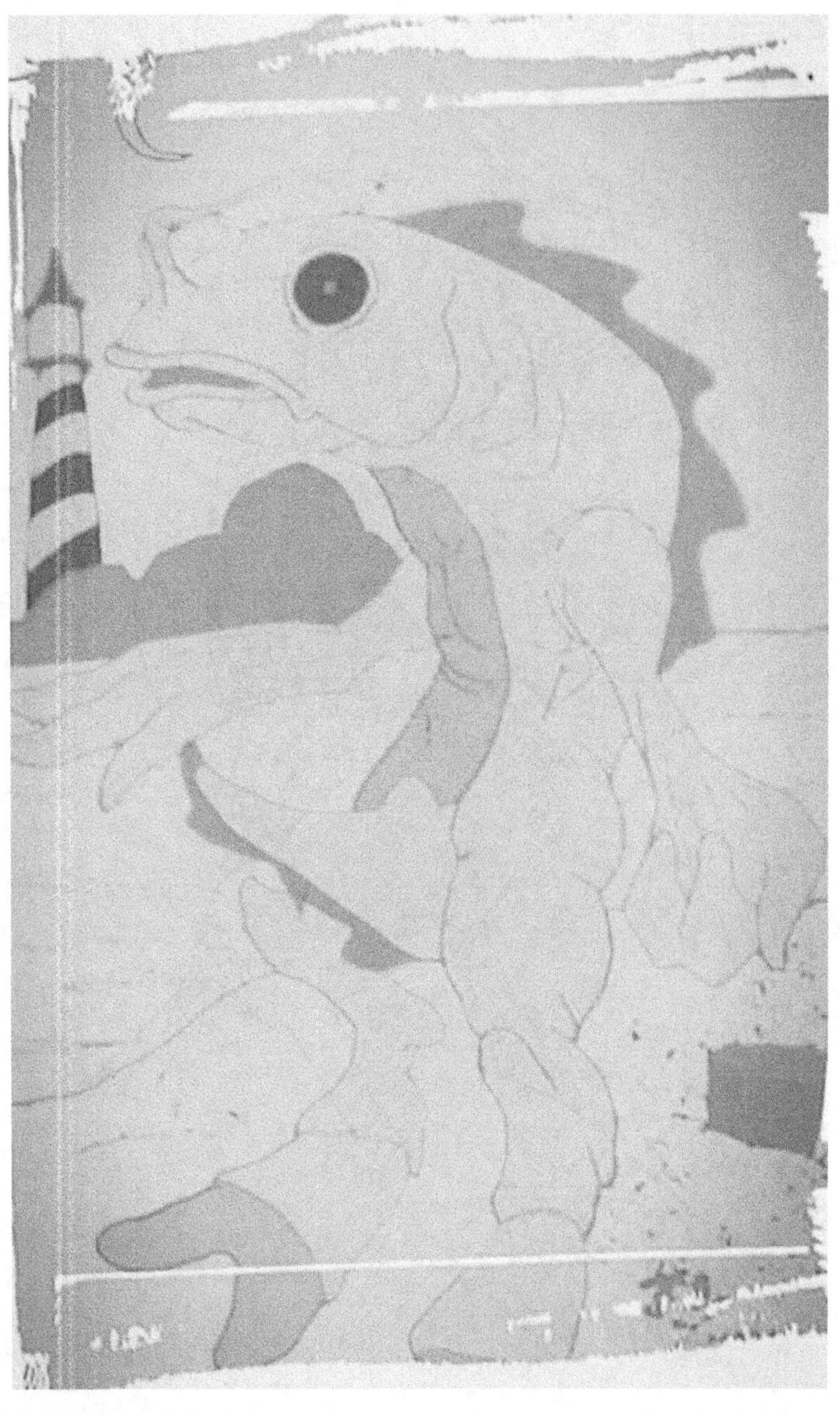

y father got up cracking his ankylosed joints, and lent me a helping hand, to do the same. I found his embrace surprisingly strong and his smile open and reassuring. We cleaned off the circle with a broom, and when even the last carbon trace was off, my mother Aisha opened her eyes and was very surprised to find us already up and dressed.

« My husband, what's happening ? ", she asked worried, « Have you been called by the malik ? Have you got a business meeting ? »

« No, my wife » Abdul Alhazred replied, smiling. « I and Ismail were not sleepy and we started chatting. That's all. »

Aisha, who when she was a girl was as thin as a willow, but getting older had become roundish, inspected suspiciously my father's face. On her chubby cheeks, you could see the dimples, which always appeared when she was disapproving something. From her face, I could understand that she was wandering if her husband had indulged in his "magic sin", as the called it, or other impious and forbidden hobbies. Poor sweet creature! She had never read a single verse of *Al Azif*. On the other hand, how could she? She was illiterate. Nor my father ever tried to explain the revelations he received. He did not think she could not understand, he just did not want to trouble her or endanger her.

«I prepared some honey cakes, yesterday evening, » Aisha said. And laid the table, after shaking Kamila and Zahira, who were still snoring despite time and people speaking.

We sat all together, eating Aisha's cakes and drinking fresh goat milk. Abdul Alhazred had also a cup of dense and fortified coffee, black and smelling good. The atmosphere was joyful and very domestic. I still remember that breakfast as one of the best moments in my whole life, despite my mother's expression sometimes indignant (she was always monitoring: she was afraid her husband could drag the children in his idolatry. And she could not forgive herself to have slept too long that morning, so that she could not know about my discussions with Abdul).

Suddenly, she asked, a bit vexed, to my father: «I've run out of eggs and pepper. Why you and Ismail don't go to the market, instead of idling and chatting like women? ».

My father seemed to accept the proposal en-
thusiastically. He got up smiling and ordered
me to follow him. «A short walk outdoor will
be nice. And I also have some business to deal
with. »

I promptly followed him and we went along
together in Damascus's streets, towards the city
place, where there was the confused market,
speckled with colours and shapes of fruits and
of lively shades of spices, clothes, pottery.

Abdul Alhazred stopped at a stand and bought
some pepper and some nutmeg. He negotiated
intensely for a long time, as only a Muslim is
able to and got, I think, the best possible price,
judging from merchant's deceived face.

People was crowding and elbowing and everyone was speaking loudly, in their gaudy caftans
and capes. My head was turning and my ears
buzzing, but I was fully satisfied and happy.

My father was in a good mood and, at a cer-
tain moment, he decided to tell me a joke. He
was used to do this often, when Aisha was not
there to blame him.

«Two officers of Malik's, arrogant and willing to have fun of someone, agreed to make
a plank to an old fearful Hebrew. They go,
armed and stiffly in their polished armours at
the old man's, who was sitting on a bench in
front of his house, washing vegetables for lung.

The officers have threatening expressions and don't say anything. In silence, they sit on the bench with the old men, without saying good morning nor asking the permission. Then, they stay there, one on the right and the other on the left, always silent and with a terrible frown. And the Hebrew is swearing and swearing, distressed and more and more nervous. When they decide their victim is ripe and ready, the officer on the right winks to the one sitting on the left and tells: "Phew! It is too hot! Hebrew, go immediately inside to bring us some lemonade!".

«The poor man gets up, trembling, and rushes inside like a greyhound. The two officers giggle and take advantage of the old man's absence to spit in his boots. Then they sit again, showing the same angry frown.

«The Hebrew comes back and gives them the lemonade. They drink it, very satisfied.

«At this point, the Hebrew puts on his boots and feels saliva under his naked feet. He understands they made fun of him. And then he says: "You know, there will be no peace possible between Muslims and Hebrew, until Muslims will not stop spitting in Hebrew's boots and Hebrew will not pissing in Muslims' lemonade.»

It was not a great joke, actually it seemed

to me quite disrespectful. However, when my father's frank laugh suddenly turned into a dreadful scream, I'd rather had listened to one hundreds like that.

I looked at him, surprised, and saw that his right arm had been torn up from his shoulder, along with cloth sleeve and that from the stump a blood fountain was shooting out. I did not know that in the human body there was such a big quantity of blood.

I screamed too, jumping by the horror. And the crowd also screamed, frozen and puzzled. All of them jumped far, like birds, trampling upon each other. Around my father, a gap was created, despite people gathering in the market. «Go away, Ismail!» Abdul Alhazred screamed, on his knees in the dust and as pale as a paper sheet. And as I stood here, unable both to help and to leave my poor, beloved father, he swore. «Go away! Run, my son, run away! Yog-Sothoth has sent one of his children to take revenge at me!»

I looked at the gap around me. There was nothing, absolutely nothing around...

Then a fruit stand broke suddenly, blowing in pieces, without any visible reason and melons and oranges were smashed and exploded. Another stand went down and another one was rudely removed. A huge round footprint ap-

peared on the pavement. And I believed to hear a strange sound, like sea undertow, or water dripping. My father's arms was torn from his place and disappeared.

My father screamed even louder and I closed my ears with my hands, my vision blurred with tears. I could not but whining: "Daddy, my daddy!".

Suddenly, Abdul Alhazred's remaining body was lifted horizontally and was broken in half. Blood and entrails squirted everywhere, on the incredulous and hysterical crowd. And my father's screams stopped. Then, piece after piece, he was swallowed and disappeared.

A piercing sound, deeper than a man can hear, filled the daylight and the dust, like a mix among trumpeting, bellowing, sea undertow and metallic vibration. And it was full of impious satisfaction. It lasted not more than thirty seconds and then went away. And nothing more happened.

Then (and only then) I obeyed my father and ran away home, fear and sorrow had made me wild and I opened a way out among fainted, petrified or panicked people.

My mother and sisters loudly whined upon hearing the terrible news. Despite the sorrow, Aisha (that incredible woman, full of resources, brave as an army general) reacted immediately. It seemed that she had feared a similar tragedy for a long time and was carefully preparing a clever solution. We left with all our belongings that night and went living in Baghdad, where my mother had made some investments, without her husband knowing, and good or bad, we succeeded in making a living and healing our wounds.

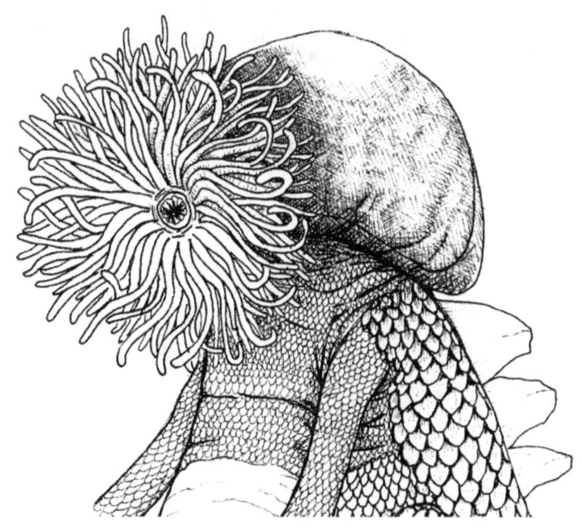

In this way, therefore, died Abdul Alhazred, known as the "Mad Arab" (actually wiser than others considered as wise nowadays). No more lessons in the magic circle for me. But I also followed in my father's footsteps and have been hindering, for years, the secret plans that the believers of that religion prepare against humankind. Will I go the same way as Abdul Alhazred? Who can tell, my children? We are all in God's hands.

# BIBLIOGRAFY


H. P. Lovecraft - *Dagon*
H. P. Lovecraft - *History of the Necronomicon*
H. P. Lovecraft - *The call of Cthulhu*
H. P. Lovecraft - *The Dream-Quest of Unknown Kadath*
H. P. Lovecraft - *The case of Charles Dexter Ward*
H. P. Lovecraft - *The shadow over Innsmouth*
H. P. Lovecraft - *The Dunwich Horror*
H. P. Lovecraft - *At the mountains of madness*
H. P. Lovecraft - *The whisperer in Darkness*
H. P. Lovecraft - *The thing on the Doorstep*
H. P. Lovecraft - *The shadow out of time*

*The Voyages and Travels of Sindbad the Sailor*, from "One thousand and One nights"

*al-Qur'ân*

*The Clavicula salomonis*

*The Grimoire of Pope Honorius*

*The hell book*

# SUMMARY

Printed on Saint Therese of Lisieux Day
October 2020
At Elves' Royal Graphic Lithography